THIS Picture Knight BOOK
BELONGS TO

....

**Mr Josiah Oldcastle
and Gumdrop**

**Farmer Herbert Puddephatt
and his Heavy Turnout**

Colonel Sir Horatio Fotheringay-Bassington
and the Silver Ghost

Grabbem Goth-Jones
and the Purple Van

GUMDROP IN DOUBLE TROUBLE

Story and pictures by Val Biro

Picture Knight

HODDER AND STOUGHTON

ONE FINE SUMMER MORNING Mr Josiah Oldcastle received a letter.

Dear Mr Oldcastle,

   On Saturday we shall hold a Children's Fancy Dress Competition at the Market House in Amersham. It would be a great honour if you would consent to meet them there and take them in your famous vintage car to the Annual Show at 3 pm.

      Yours sincerely,
      Horsefield McFarland
      Chairman of the Show

Mr Oldcastle looked at his famous vintage car. It was an Austin Clifton Heavy Twelve-four, vintage 1926, and it was called Gumdrop.

"Come on, Horace!" called Mr Oldcastle to his dog, "the Show is held this very afternoon and we must polish Gumdrop first."

Horace wagged his
tail, the sun shone,
the birds sang and all
was well with the world.

Mr Oldcastle washed the body down first and leathered it
until it shone. Then he polished the windscreen. Next he
lifted the bonnet and polished the carburettor,

 the dynamo and 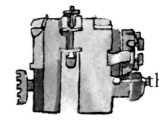 the magneto.

He then polished all the things made of brass:

the radiator, 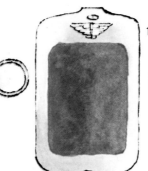 the thermometer,

the lamps 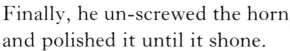 and the driving mirror.

Finally, he un-screwed the horn
and polished it until it shone.

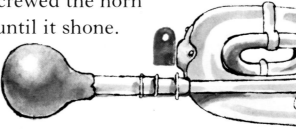

Just then a purple van stopped by the gate and a man got out. "Goth-Jones is the name," he said, "scrap-merchant." He pointed at Gumdrop. "Is this old crock for sale? I might buy it, though it's not much more than a scrapheap on wheels."

An old crock! A scrapheap! Gumdrop has never been so insulted. Mr Oldcastle was furious, but he remained icily polite.

"I am afraid my car is not for sale, and I am in a hurry just now. If you will therefore excuse me, sir, I'll bid you good day." And with that he turned and went into the house.

When he came out again, Goth-Jones had left.
"Jump in, Horace, we are off!" Mr Oldcastle switched
on the engine and swung the starting-handle.

But Gumdrop wouldn't start. Everything was in order
but there was no spark.

The magneto had broken down. And the children
were waiting, and would miss the Show!

Just then,
Mr Puddephatt appeared,
driving his great Shire horses to the Show.
"My magneto has broken down," called Mr Oldcastle,
"but we can start the engine if you would kindly give me a tow."

So the horses were hitched to Gumdrop. Thudder and
Thumper were strong, and they pulled at a smart trot. The
engine coughed and roared into life. But Mr Puddephatt
looked miserable as he unhitched the horses.
"That's all very well," he said, "but my brass lamps are
missing. I think there must be a thief around."

Mr Oldcastle was very sorry to hear this but he was in a hurry to meet the children. So he thanked Mr Puddephatt and he reached for the horn as he drove off. But the horn wasn't there – it wasn't anywhere.

There must have been a thief around! Goth-Jones! – he must have stolen it!!

"I know that thief who stole your lamps," he shouted, "he drove that way in a purple van!" Mr Puddephatt jumped into Gumdrop. "After him, by George!" he yelled and they drove off.

The purple van wasn't far ahead, and they drove on in pursuit. But round a bend they were held up by The Best Car In the World. Colonel Sir Horatio Fotheringay-Bassington looked miserable.

"The Silver Lady from my radiator is missing. Have you seen a thief hereabouts?"

"Yes," said Mr Oldcastle, "and we are chasing him."

The Colonel jumped into
his Rolls-Royce Silver Ghost.
"After him, by Jove!" he
commanded, and both cars drove off.

And suddenly there, a little way ahead, was the purple van! Gumdrop was catching up fast. Goth-Jones panicked. He stopped the van, jumped out and ran into a field.

But there came Balthazar, the bull, to chase
Goth-Jones out again! And there was Horace
running after the bull! And there came
Mr Oldcastle to catch Horace, and
there were others running
after the lot of them!!

But Goth-Jones was too quick. He doubled back to his van and drove off. Balthazar doubled back too, jumped off the edge, and landed right on Gumdrop's back seat. And there he stuck.

And Gumdrop's engine stopped.

"Push-start! Push-start!" shouted Mr Oldcastle in excitement. There was no time to lift Balthazar out of Gumdrop – anyway he looked very happy there. So the others pushed Gumdrop until the engine started again.

But where was Horace? "I saw him chasing the thief into his van!" said Mr Puddephatt. "After him, by Gum!" growled Mr Oldcastle grimly as he drove on again.

Gumdrop was in double trouble now.

And then they saw
the purple van again.
It was at Amersham and there, too,
were the children waiting outside the
Market House. So Gumdrop had to stop.
"Quick! We're after that thief!" shouted
Mr Oldcastle. The children piled into Gumdrop.
"A thief! A chase! Hooray!!" they shouted.
They didn't mind Balthazar – anyway he was asleep.

The chase went on for miles until, at last, they caught up with the purple van again. And there was the entrance to the Show! Goth-Jones couldn't stop, so he drove right in. And Gumdrop and the Ghost drove in right after him.

And there they were, chasing the purple van round and round the ring. People thought it was a pretend chase and they all cheered.

But when they dashed out of the ring again, Gumdrop's engine coughed, spluttered and stopped. The magneto had finally broken down. Gumdrop was in real trouble.

"Catch that van!" roared the Colonel. They all jumped out and ran after the van. There were such crowds that the purple van had to stop too. Goth-Jones jumped out and they all chased him. He ran one way – and there was the Colonel. He ran the other way – and there were the children. He then ran back towards Gumdrop – and there was Balthazar.

Balthazar woke up, un-stuck himself and clambered out
of Gumdrop. He recognised Goth-Jones, and roared.
The thief was terrified. He turned back again –
and ran straight into the arms
of a large policeman.
And he was caught.
The chase was over.

They went back to the purple van to search it. There, sure enough, the Colonel found the Silver Lady under the seat, and Mr Puddephatt found the brass lamps in the back. Mr Oldcastle looked too, but he found nothing. No horn. No Horace. He was miserable as he walked back to Gumdrop. And no magneto now, either. Gumdrop was in treble trouble now!

Just then, he heard a familiar bark. The unmistakable bark of Horace – coming from Gumdrop! And there was Horace – with Gumdrop's shiny brass horn in his paws!

Mr Oldcastle was delighted. His clever hound had waited in the van until Goth-Jones had jumped out. He had found the horn in the van, recognised it, taken it in his mouth and brought it straight back to Gumdrop.

The others came back too and congratulated Mr Oldcastle on his good fortune.

"I understand, however, that your splendid vehicle is having magneto trouble," said the Colonel. "We can't have that, by Jove! It so happens that I have a brand new spare magneto in my Ghost. Permit me to present it to you as a small recompense for your valiant efforts."

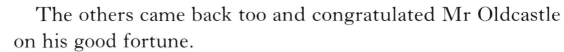

A new magneto for Gumdrop! This will make Gumdrop go again. And there and then Mr Oldcastle got to work. It was a job for three men and a dog.

So the Colonel took out the broken magneto.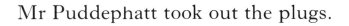

Mr Puddephatt took out the plugs.

Mr Oldcastle then strapped the new magneto securely in place, and Horace fetched the spanner.

To time the ignition, they had to do everything at once.

The Colonel turned the starting-handle, Mr Puddephatt looked at the flywheel, Mr Oldcastle checked the contact-breaker, and when everything was in order, Horace barked.

The plugs went back, the leads were attached and the job was done. Would Gumdrop start?
Mr Oldcastle switched on and swung the starting-handle. Gumdrop's engine started to purr at once, and it purred more sweetly than ever!

Mr Oldcastle thanked everybody and got into Gumdrop.
As they drove off, Horace gave a happy bark, and
Mr Oldcastle honked the horn. His troubles were over.
And Gumdrop's trouble was over, too.

British Library Cataloguing in Publication Data

Biro, Val
    Gumdrop in double trouble.
    Rn: Balint Stephan Biro   I. Title
    823.914[J]

    ISBN 0-340-42391-9

First published 1975 by Hodder and Stoughton Children's Books
Picture Knight edition first published 1988
Third impression 1990

Published by Hodder and Stoughton Children's Books,
a division of Hodder and Stoughton Ltd,
Mill Road, Dunton Green, Sevenoaks, Kent TN13 2YA
Editorial office: 47 Bedford Square, London WC1E 3DP

Printed in Great Britain by Springbourne Press Limited,
Basildon, Essex

Other Gumdrop titles published in Picture Knight:

Gumdrop Makes a Start
Gumdrop on the Rally